The Usborne Big Book of Fairy things to make and do

Fiona Watt, Rebecca Gilpin
and Leonie Pratt

Designed and illustrated by Katrina Fearn,
Jan McCafferty, Antonia Miller, Lucy Parris
and Josephine Thompson

Additional design by Stella Baggott
and Katie Lovell

Photographs by Howard Allman

Contents

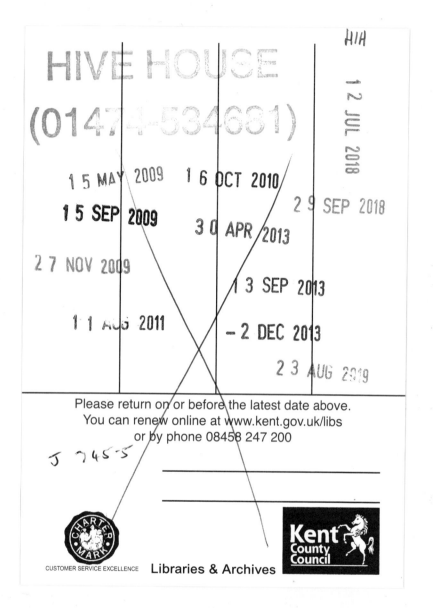

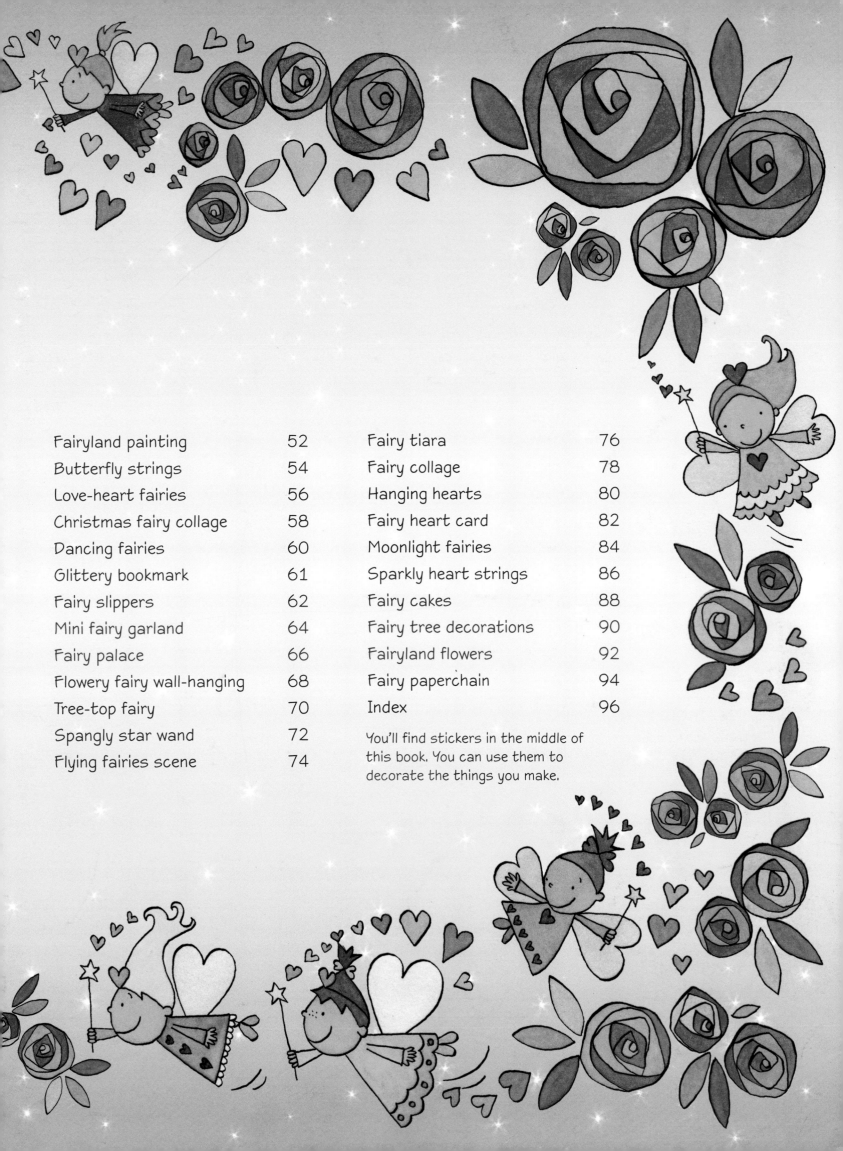

You'll find stickers in the middle of this book. You can use them to decorate the things you make.

Pretty fairies

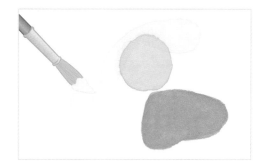

1. Use watery paint to paint a circle on a piece of paper for the fairy's face. Then, paint a simple shape beneath it for her dress.

2. Paint a wing on either side of the dress with watery paint. Paint the hair and a dot for the wand. Leave the paint to dry.

3. Draw around the chin, dress and wings with a black felt-tip pen. You don't have to stick to the painted shapes exactly.

Paint lots of flowers and fairies together, like these, to make a big fairy picture.

4. Draw her eyes, nose and mouth, then add lines in her hair. Draw her arms, making them overlap the wings. Then, draw a wand.

5. For a flower, paint large petals with watery paint. Add another blob of thicker paint on top, for the middle of the flower.

6. When the paint is dry, draw around the middle of the flower with a black felt-tip pen. Then, add petals around the edge.

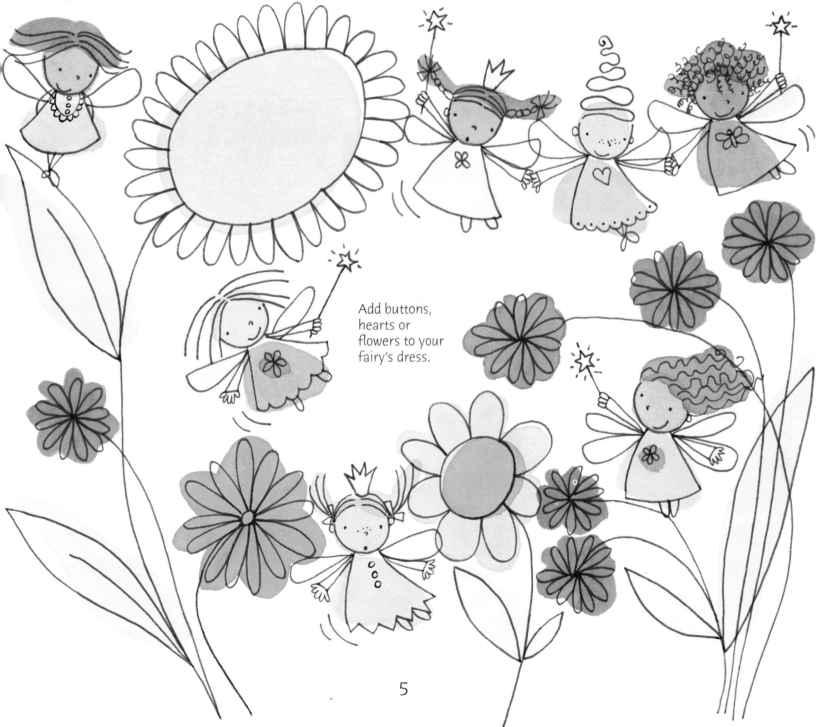

Add buttons, hearts or flowers to your fairy's dress.

Fairy door sign

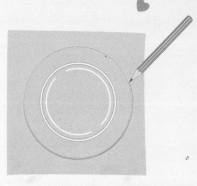

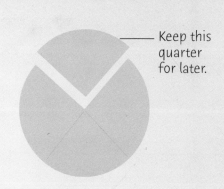

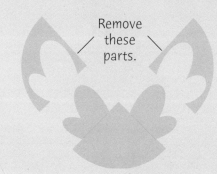

Keep this quarter for later.

Remove these parts.

1. Put a small plate onto a sheet of paper and draw around it with a pencil. Then, cut out the circle you have drawn.

2. Fold the circle in half, then in half again, and open it out. Then, cut along two of the folds and remove one quarter.

3. Draw two wings touching the folds. Then, cut around the wings and along the folds to make the wings, like this.

Kate's Room

The body stands out from the paper.

4. Decorate the body and the wings. Push the wings together, so the body curves, then glue them onto some thick paper.

5. Cut out a head and draw a face. Then, cut out hair and glue it on. Draw two arms on the paper quarter you kept earlier.

Asha's Room

You could glue your fairy onto a heart. Leave room to write your name.

Decorate the sign with shiny stickers.

Decorate the arms.

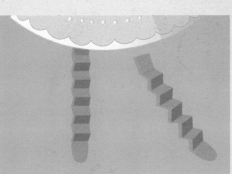

6. Cut out the arms. Then, cut out hands and glue them onto the arms. Glue the arms and the head onto the body.

7. For legs, cut two long strips of paper. Make one end of each leg rounded, then fold the legs lots of times, to make zigzags.

8. Glue the legs under the body, with the rounded ends at the bottom. Then, write your name above the fairy.

Ice fairies

1. Pour some white paint onto an old plate. Then, cut a rectangle from thick cardboard and dip one edge into the paint.

2. To make a skirt, place the edge of the cardboard on some paper. Scrape it around, keeping the top end in the same place.

3. To make the body, dip the edge of a shorter piece of cardboard into the paint. Then, place it above the skirt and drag it across.

4. Mix some paint for the skin. Then, dip the end of another piece of cardboard into the paint. Press it onto the paper, to print arms.

5. Cut a small cardboard rectangle and print a neck and two feet. Then, dip your fingertip into the paint and print a head.

6. When the head is dry, spread a little blue paint onto the plate. Then, dip your finger into the paint and fingerprint some hair.

You could decorate the fairies'
skirts with a line of glitter glue.

The part you're holding
will stay sticky.

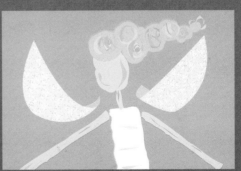

7. For the wings, sprinkle
a little glitter onto some
newspaper. Hold a piece
of sticky tape at one end
and dip it into the glitter.

8. Dip a second piece of
tape into the glitter. Then,
cut a corner off each piece
of tape, away from the
sticky end, like this.

9. Press the sticky end of
the wings onto the fairy.
Then, fold them back and
press them down, so that
the glitter is on the front.

Fairy wands

Sparkly star wand

1. Draw a star on a piece of cardboard. Cut it out, then lay it on another piece of cardboard and draw around it twice.

2. Cut out the stars and paint them on one side. Then, cut 10 pieces of thin ribbon which are half as long as a drinking straw.

3. Lay one of the stars on some scrap paper. Then, cover the side which has not been painted with white glue.

4. Carefully lay the straw and pieces of ribbon on top of the glue, like this. Then, gently glue the other star on top.

The paper protects the book.

5. Lay a sheet of paper over the star. Then, put a heavy book on top, and leave the wand for an hour for the glue to dry.

6. Glue lots of sequins, glitter and tiny beads onto one side of the wand. Wait for it to dry, then decorate the other side.

Silver star wand

1. Cut out two stars and cover one side of each one with white glue. Then, press pieces of string onto the glue.

2. Lay a piece of kitchen foil over each star and gently rub all over it. The pattern of the pieces of string appears.

3. When the glue is dry, cut around the stars, leaving a border. Then, cut off the foil at the points, like this.

4. Cut little triangles into the border, like this. Then, bend the border up onto the star, until the edges of the star are covered.

5. Glue pieces of ribbon and a straw onto the back of one star. Then, glue the other star on the top and leave it to dry.

Funky fairies

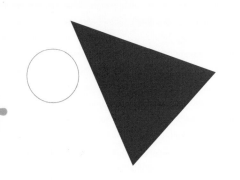

1. Cut a round head shape from thin cardboard. Then, cut a triangle from bright cardboard, for the fairy's body.

2. Cut two bright paper triangles for hair. Then, cut curves along the bottom edges and round off the points at the top.

3. Glue the head onto the body, and glue the hair onto the head, so that the pieces touch at the top. Then, draw a face.

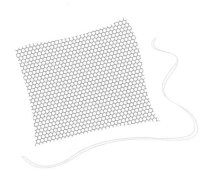

4. Cut a square of pink net for the fairy's wings. Then, cut a long piece of bright ribbon to hang the fairy from.

5. Scrunch the middle of the netting and tie it with one end of the ribbon. Then, cut two long pieces of ribbon, for legs.

6. Turn the body over, and tape the wings onto it, with the long piece of ribbon pointing up. Then, tape the legs on, too.

You could make lots
of different fairies.

7. To make the arms, bend the bumpy part of a drinking straw and cut it so that both ends are the same length, like this.

8. Press the bumpy part of the straw onto a piece of poster tack. Then, press it onto the back of the fairy, just above the wings.

9. For feet, thread beads onto the fairy's legs and tie knots below them. Then, press a sticker on her hair and hang her up.

Printed fairies

To make a butterfly, cut wings from paper and fold them.

1. Glue a sponge cloth onto a piece of thin cardboard. This helps to make it less messy when you print.

2. Draw a triangle for the body on the cardboard. Then, put a small bottle top on the cardboard and draw around it.

3. Cut around the shapes, through the cardboard and the sponge. Then, lay some paper towels onto some newspaper.

4. Spread white paint on the paper towels, using the back of an old spoon. Then, lay the sponge side of the triangle in the paint.

14

5. Press the sponge onto a sheet of paper, rub the back gently, then lift it off. Then, print a head and print more fairies.

6. From thin paper, cut enough wing shapes for each fairy to have two. Then, fold each wing in half and open it out.

7. Mix yellow and white paint together to make pale yellow. Then, press the edge of a piece of thick cardboard into the paint.

Leave room for the wings.

The wings stand out a little.

8. Press the cardboard onto the paper to print hair. Then, use another piece of cardboard to print arms and legs.

9. Paint hands and feet, and add faces. Then, spread glue on one half of each wing, and press them on.

To give a fairy curved legs or arms, bend the cardboard before you print.

15

Sparkly fairy wings

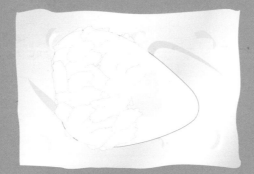

1. Draw two big wing shapes and two smaller ones on paper. Then, cut them out and lay plastic food wrap over them.

2. Rip up white tissue paper and lay the pieces overlapping on the food wrap. Cover the shapes, including their edges.

3. Mix some white glue with water so that it is runny. Then, brush the glue over the pieces of tissue paper.

4. Rip pieces of pink tissue paper, lay them on top, then brush them with glue. Add two more layers of white tissue paper and glue.

Put the wings on your back and ask someone to tie the ribbons around your arms at the front.

5. Sprinkle glitter over the wet glue on the wings. Let it dry, then brush another layer of glue over the top of the glitter. Leave it to dry.

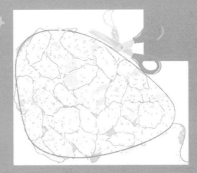

6. Peel the wings off the foodwrap. Lay the paper wing shapes on top, then draw around them. Cut out the shapes you have drawn.

These wings had curves cut in the wing shapes in step 1.

7. Glue the top parts of the wings onto the bottom parts. Decorate the wings with sequins, stickers or shiny paper shapes.

Use a ballpoint pen.

8. Cut a small rectangle from thick cardboard. Make four holes in it with a pen, then thread two long pieces of ribbon through the holes.

Leave long ends on the ribbons.

9. Glue the rectangle onto the back of the wings, with the ends of the ribbons sticking out. Then, let the glue dry completely.

17

Fairy flower chains

Tape the flowers onto a window, so that the light shines through them.

1. Lay a large piece of plastic foodwrap on an old magazine. Then, rip two shades of pink tissue paper into lots of pieces.

2. Lay pieces of tissue paper on the foodwrap, overlapping each other. Cover as much of the foodwrap as you can.

3. Mix some white glue with water so that it is runny. Paint glue over the pieces of tissue paper, until they are covered.

4. Add another layer of tissue paper and glue. Then, add a third layer of paper and glue, and sprinkle glitter on the top.

5. When the glue is dry, paint glue over the glitter and let it dry. Then, lay another piece of foodwrap on a newspaper.

6. Make layers of orange and yellow tissue paper and glue, as you did before. Add glitter and glue and leave it to dry.

18

You could make lots of chains and hang them up.

You could put sparkly flowers into a card so that they tumble out when it's opened.

7. Peel the glittery tissue paper off the foodwrap. Then, cut out pink flowers and small pink circles. Cut out some orange ones too.

8. Glue the orange circles onto the middle of the pink flowers. Glue pink circles onto the middle of the orange flowers.

9. Then, cut some thin ribbon into pieces which are different lengths and tape the flowers onto the ribbons, to make a chain.

Fairy flower garden

1. Cut out pages with lots of pictures of pretty flowers from old magazines. Then, cut around individual flowers and some leaves.

2. Glue the flowers onto a piece of paper. Make some of the flowers overlap. Leave spaces between some of them, for the fairies.

Draw one or two fairies flying between flowers.

If you draw your fairy with her arms in the air it makes her look as if she is waving or jumping up.

 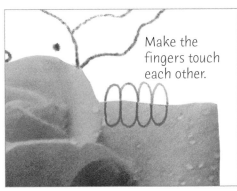 

3. Draw the top part of a fairy's face peeking out over the top of a flower. Add the eyes and nose only. Then, draw the hair, too.

4. For fingers, draw four long ovals. Make them overlap the edge of the flower to look as if they are curling over the petal.

Make the fingers touch each other.

5. You could also draw a fairy looking around the side of a flower. Just draw part of her body - the rest of it is hidden.

You could draw around the wings with a blue felt-tip pen.

6. When you have drawn your fairies, fill them in with felt-tip pens or paints. Then, draw around them with a black pen.

Glue leaves under some flowers.

Fairy crown

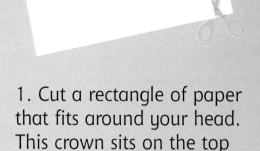

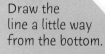

Draw the line a little way from the bottom.

Use hair clips to clip the crown to your hair.

1. Cut a rectangle of paper that fits around your head. This crown sits on the top of your head, so cut a little off one end.

2. Fold the rectangle in half, with the short ends together, then fold it twice more. Then, draw a line across the paper, like this.

Crease mark

Cut through all the layers.

3. To mark the middle of the folded paper, fold it in half, with the long sides together. Then, press it to make a crease at the end.

4. Using a ruler, draw a line from the crease mark to each end of the line at the bottom. Then, cut along the slanting lines.

5. Unfold the paper shape, then lay it on a piece of thin cardboard. Carefully draw around the shape, and cut it out.

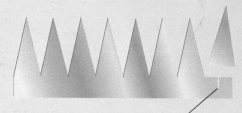

The cut goes halfway down.

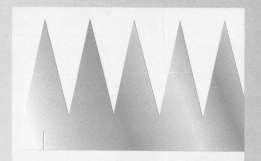

6. Cut off the triangle at one end, leaving a strip at the bottom. Then, make a cut down into the strip, like this.

7. At the other end of the crown, make a cut up into the last triangle, like this. Make the cut the same length as the first one.

8. Bend the crown around and slot the cuts into each other, with the ends inside. Then, secure the ends with a piece of tape.

Glue little beads onto
the ends of the points.

9. Bend each point out
with your fingers, like this.
Then, glue beads and
sequins onto the crown, or
decorate it with glitter glue.

23

Fairyland butterflies

Salt-speckled butterflies

1. Paint all over a sheet of thick white paper with watery paint. Then, sprinkle grains of salt onto the paint and let it dry.

2. When the paint is dry, brush off the salt. Fold the paper in half and glue it together with the paint on the outside.

The fold needs to be on this side.

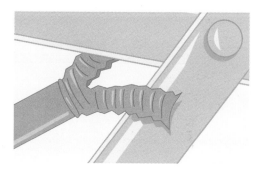

3. Fold the paper in half again. Draw two butterfly wings on it, then cut around the wings, through all the layers of paper.

4. For each butterfly, cut the end off a drinking straw, just above the bumpy part. To make feelers, cut down into the bumpy part.

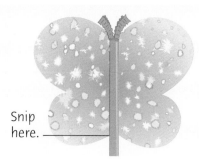

Snip here.

Make sure the bead is wider than the straw.

5. Bend the feelers outward, then open the wings. Lay the straw in the fold, then snip off the bottom end of the straw.

6. Push a piece of ribbon through a bead. Tie a knot in the ribbon and push it through the straw. Glue the straw onto the wings.

Make lots of
butterflies, then
hang them up.

Splattered butterflies

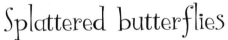

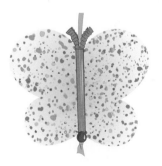

1. Paint all over a sheet of thick white paper with watery paint and let it dry. Then, put some bright paint on an old plate.

2. Dip a dry paintbrush into the paint, then hold it over the paper. Pull a finger over the bristles, to splatter the paint.

3. Splatter paint all over the paper and let it dry. Then, make two butterflies, following the steps on the opposite page.

Mini fairy love tokens

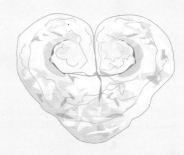

1. Cut a piece of kitchen foil that is about the size of this page. Then, scrunch it tightly in the middle, like this.

2. To make one side of the heart, gently scrunch one end of the foil in on itself. Then, bend it around, into the middle of the foil.

3. Scrunch the other end of the foil in the same way. Then, bend it around into the middle, to make a heart shape.

Lay the heart on some plastic foodwrap.

4. Press the heart with your hands, to squash the foil into a smooth shape. Make a point at the bottom of the heart.

5. Rip a piece of bright tissue paper into lots of small pieces. Then, brush part of the foil heart with white glue.

Try gluing on sequins or little paper shapes.

This heart was decorated with tiny beads.

6. Press pieces of tissue paper onto the wet glue. Then, brush on more glue and press on more paper, until the heart is covered.

Lay the heart on a newspaper.

7. Leave the glue to dry completely. Then, mix some bright paint and white glue together well on an old plate.

8. Paint decorations on the heart with a thin paintbrush. Sprinkle glitter over the wet paint, shake off any excess and let it dry.

Fairy ice castle

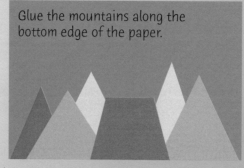
Glue the mountains along the bottom edge of the paper.

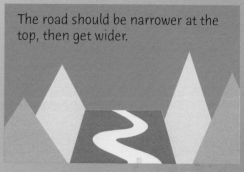
The road should be narrower at the top, then get wider.

1. For the mountains, cut different shades of pink paper into different sizes of triangles. Make one bigger than all the others.

2. Cut the top off the biggest triangle. Glue the other mountains onto a large piece of blue paper. Glue the big one on last.

3. On a piece of pale pink paper, draw a wiggly road to go on the big mountain. Cut out the shape you have drawn and glue it on.

Draw small windows in silver felt-tip pen.

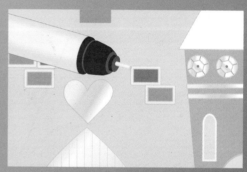

4. Cut out three very tall towers and glue them on. Cut out a wall and glue it on. Then, cut out and glue on two short towers.

5. Cut out triangles from shiny paper for the roofs and glue them on. Cut out and glue on a door and windows, too.

6. Decorate the castle with sequins and shiny shapes. Draw bricks, and outline the bricks and the windows with a silver felt-tip pen.

7. Pour some granulated sugar and a little glitter into a container. Then, shake the container so that they mix together.

8. Dab white glue onto the road, the mountains and the roofs. Pour the sugar mixture on, then tap off any excess.

Cut out a foil shape for the moon and decorate the sky with stars from the sticker pages.

Rainy day fairies

Leave space on your paper to draw more fairies.

The crayon lines are shown here in yellow so that you can see them.

1. Use a pencil to draw a circle for the fairy's head. Then, add a dress with a wavy bottom edge. Draw her arms, legs and wings.

2. Draw her hair, eyes and eyelashes, her nose and a big smile. Then, draw little heart-shaped lips. Add a wand in her hand.

3. Draw more fairies in the same way. Add some leaves and toadstools, as umbrellas. Use a white wax crayon to draw lines for raindrops.

You could draw flowers and stars around your fairies and add some creatures, too.

The raindrops show through the paint.

4. Brush water over the paper. Then, brush watery pink paint on top so that it spreads in the water. Add some blobs of yellow paint.

5. When the paint is dry, draw over all your pencil lines with different felt-tip pens. Add patterns on the fairies' dresses, too.

6. Dip a thin paintbrush into water, then brush it over the pen lines so that the ink runs. Clean your brush after you do each part.

You could draw a heart, instead of a star, on the end of a wand.

One fairy could be wearing a pair of glasses.

Snowflake fairies

1. Lay a mug on a piece of white paper. Draw around it, then draw around it on some purple paper, too. Then, cut out the circles.

2. To make a snowflake for the dress, fold the white circle in half, then fold it in half twice more. Then, cut a triangle out of one side.

3. Cut out lots more triangles, all around the edges of the folded piece of paper. Make the triangles different sizes.

4. Brush white glue over the snowflake. Sprinkle it with glitter, then let it dry. Then, glue it onto the purple circle.

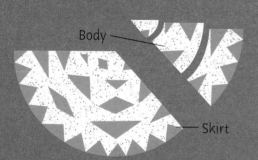

Body

Skirt

5. Cut the snowflake in half. For a skirt, cut one half into two pieces. Then, cut a shape for the body from the smaller piece.

6. Glue the skirt onto a piece of paper, then glue on the body. Cut out a purple sash and glue it on, where the pieces join.

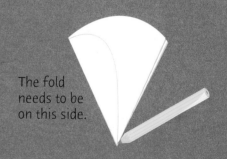

The fold needs to be on this side.

7. For the wings, draw around the mug and cut out the circle. Fold it in half three times, then draw half a wing shape, like this.

You could make a
Christmas card with a
snowflake fairy on it.

Keep the
paper folded.

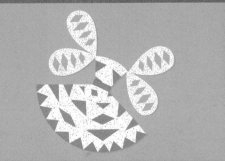

Add glittery
shoes,
too.

8. Cut along the line you have drawn, then cut a few triangles along the fold, like this. Then, open out the wings.

9. Spread glue over the wings. Sprinkle them with glitter, then let the glue dry. Glue the wings next to the body, like this.

10. Cut out a head and some hair and glue them together. Cut out arms, legs and a crown and glue them all on. Then, draw a face.

Flying fairy card

Make sure both cuts are the same length.

1. Cut two rectangles of paper the same size, one blue and one green. Fold the green rectangle in half so the short edges meet.

2. Make two small cuts in the middle of the folded edge, to make a flap. Crease the flap to the front, then to the back.

3. Open the card and push the flap through the card, like this. Close the card and smooth it flat, then open it again.

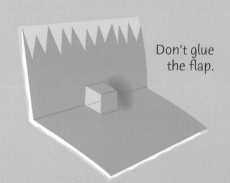

4. For the grass, draw a zigzag line across the card, above the flap. Then, cut along the line you have drawn, like this.

Don't glue the flap.

Decorate the flowers with glitter and sequins to make them more sparkly.

5. For the sky, fold the blue paper in half. Then, glue the green card onto it, making sure that the middle folds line up.

34

Shake off any excess glitter.

6. For the fairy, cut out some wings and spread white glue over them. Sprinkle them with glitter and let them dry.

7. For the fairy's head, cut a circle from pink paper. Cut out a shape for her hair, then glue it onto the head. Draw a face.

To make your card even more sparkly, add a glittery sun and clouds.

8. Cut out shapes for her dress, arms and feet. Glue the arms and feet onto the back of the dress and glue the head onto the front.

9. Dab glue on the wings and press them onto the back of her dress. Then, decorate the fairy with sequins and glitter glue.

10. Glue the fairy onto the top of the flap. Then, decorate the card by cutting out flowers and gluing them onto the grass.

Glittery star chains

Cut the paper at an angle, like this.

1. To make a star, put a mug on a piece of paper and draw around it with a pencil. Then, cut out the circle you have drawn.

2. Fold the circle in half, then fold it in half three more times. Then, cut across the folded piece of paper, to make a point.

The dot shows you which point you folded first.

3. Unfold the star. Draw a pencil dot on one of the points. Then, fold the star in half from this point to the point opposite it.

4. Crease the fold, then open out the star. Fold the next point over to the point opposite it. Then, fold the others in the same way.

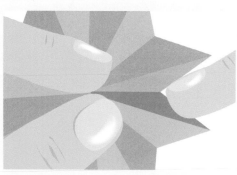

Press lightly, or you will squash the star.

5. To make a dip between two points, push the points together. Squash down the fold between them. Repeat this all the way around.

6. Unfold the star and gently press down on its middle, to open out the points a little. Then, make more stars for the chain.

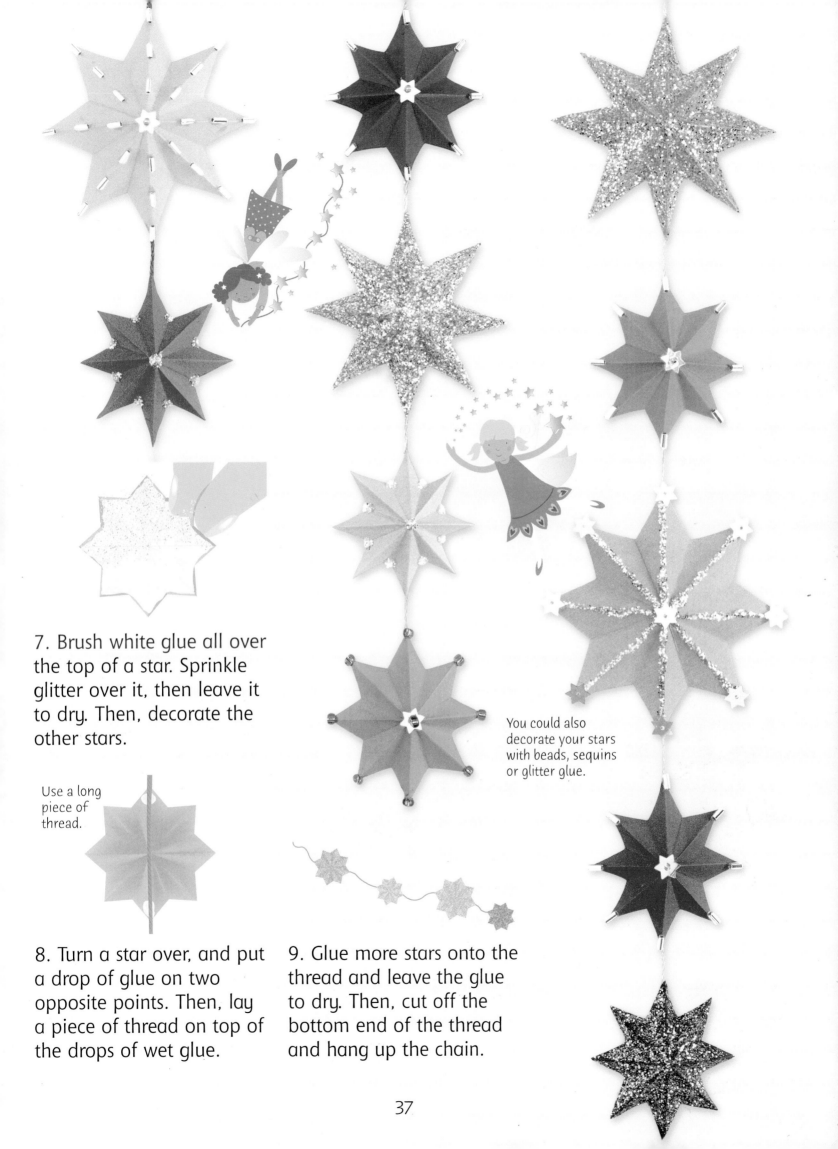

7. Brush white glue all over the top of a star. Sprinkle glitter over it, then leave it to dry. Then, decorate the other stars.

Use a long piece of thread.

8. Turn a star over, and put a drop of glue on two opposite points. Then, lay a piece of thread on top of the drops of wet glue.

9. Glue more stars onto the thread and leave the glue to dry. Then, cut off the bottom end of the thread and hang up the chain.

You could also decorate your stars with beads, sequins or glitter glue.

37

Flying fairies

Paint a big pond, then add lots of fairies flying around.

You could draw some fairies standing on lily pads.

Paint the hair overlapping the head a little.

Make the wings overlap.

Draw the stick of the wand on either side of her hand.

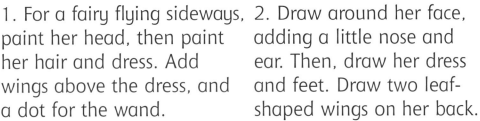

1. For a fairy flying sideways, paint her head, then paint her hair and dress. Add wings above the dress, and a dot for the wand.

2. Draw around her face, adding a little nose and ear. Then, draw her dress and feet. Draw two leaf-shaped wings on her back.

3. Draw one arm on the dress and the other one below her face. Then, draw a stick for the wand. Add a star, and wavy lines for hair.

Looking around

You can make your fairy look up or down by drawing her eyes, nose and mouth in different places on her face.

For looking down, draw the eyes in the middle, and the mouth and nose at the bottom.

To make a fairy look up, draw her eyes and nose near the top of her head. Draw the mouth in the middle.

Glittery winged unicorns

1. Dip your finger in white paint and fingerpaint around and around for a body. Fingerpaint a head and a line for the neck.

2. For the legs, cut a strip of cardboard. Then, dip one of the long sides in the paint and drag it across the paper three times.

3. For a bent leg, dip a smaller piece of cardboard in the paint and drag two lines. Use a corner of the cardboard to paint the ears.

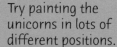

Try painting the unicorns in lots of different positions.

These unicorns had glitter lightly sprinkled over them while the paint was still wet.

4. Squeeze a line of glitter glue along the unicorn's neck. Then, use a corner of the cardboard to drag curved lines for the mane.

5. Squeeze more lines of glitter glue for the tail and drag them with the cardboard to make them wispy. Then, add a horn.

6. When the glitter glue has dried, use a black felt-tip pen to draw the unicorn's eye, nostril and mouth.

Dip the tape in the glitter so that one end stays sticky.

7. For the sparkly wings, sprinkle some glitter onto a plate. Cut two pieces of sticky tape and dip each one in the glitter.

8. Press the sticky ends of the tape onto the unicorn's back. Fold up the glittery parts, then cut the corners off so they look like wings.

Fairyland caterpillar and flowers

Caterpillar

You don't need the lid.

1. Carefully cut the lid off a cardboard egg carton. Then, cut the bottom part of the carton into two pieces, along its length.

2. To make the caterpillar, paint one piece green, and leave it to dry. Put the other piece to one side, for the flowers.

3. Carefully push the point of a ballpoint pen into the front of the caterpillar to make two holes for its feelers.

4. Push two short pieces of drinking straw through the holes. Then, draw a face. Press stickers all over the caterpillar's body.

You could paint spots instead of using stickers.

Make flowers with different petal shapes.

Flowers

1. For the middles of the flowers, cut the other piece of egg carton into three pieces. Paint them orange and let them dry.

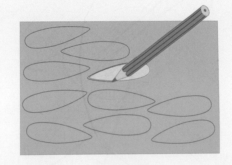

2. Draw a petal on thin cardboard and cut it out. Then, draw around it lots of times on bright paper and cut out the shapes.

3. Turn the orange pieces over and glue the petals onto them, overlapping the petals a little. Then, leave the glue to dry.

4. Scrunch up three pieces of yellow tissue paper. Then, glue them into the middles of the orange sections.

5. For the stalks, press a piece of poster tack onto the back of each flower. Then, press a straw into the poster tack.

Painted fairy card

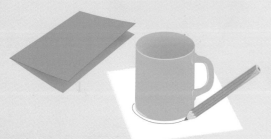

1. For the card, fold a piece of blue paper in half. Then, lay a mug on a piece of white paper. Draw around it, then cut out the circle.

2. Mix some paint for the fairy's face and body. Paint a face on the circle. Then, paint a body below it, like this.

3. Paint four shapes for the fairy's wings. Then, paint the hair and a small yellow circle for the end of the wand.

You could paint little white dots around the circle instead.

Try painting fairies with their wands and arms in different positions.

44

4. When the paint is dry, outline the fairy's body, chin and wings with a black felt-tip pen. Decorate her dress, too.

5. Draw a face, then add arms, legs and lines on the fairy's hair. Then, draw a wand with a star on the end, like this.

6. Glue the circle onto the folded card. Then, paint a thin white line down from the top of the card and add a bow.

You could print a mixture of patterns and dots on the card.

7. To print the patterns, cut a small piece of thick cardboard. Dip the end of it into some white paint, then press it onto the card.

8. Print a second line across the first one and add a third line. Print lots more patterns around the circle.

Sparkling boxes

1. Mix some white glue with a little water. Then, cut some bright tissue paper into lots of small pieces.

2. Brush the glue over a box and its lid. Then, while the glue is wet, press pieces of tissue paper all over the box, making them overlap.

Try brushing different shapes, such as stars, onto the lids.

You can put another layer of paper on before the first one has dried.

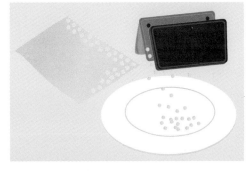

3. Brush on another layer of glue and press on more tissue paper. Add a few more layers, then leave the glue to dry.

4. To make shiny paper sequins, punch lots of holes in a piece of shiny paper. Then, empty the hole puncher onto a plate.

5. With the tip of a small paintbrush, dab little blobs of glue around the edge of the lid. Then, press the sequins onto the glue.

6. Brush a spiral of glue on the lid. Then, sprinkle glitter over the glue and shake off any excess. Let the glue dry.

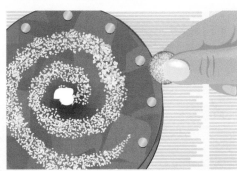

7. To make a sparkly gem, dip a piece of tissue paper in the glue and roll it into a ball. Then, roll the ball in some glitter.

8. Leave the sparkly gem to dry. Then, dab a blob of glue in the middle of the spiral and press the gem onto the glue.

Fairy pop-up card

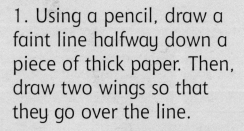

Don't press hard.

1. Using a pencil, draw a faint line halfway down a piece of thick paper. Then, draw two wings so that they go over the line.

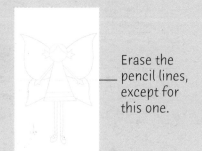

Erase the pencil lines, except for this one.

2. Pressing lightly, draw a body and a head. Add hair, arms and legs. Then, outline the fairy with a felt-tip pen, like this.

Glue on sequins and tiny beads, too, if you like.

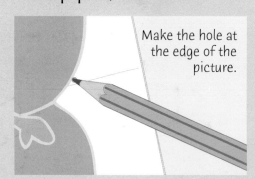

Make the hole at the edge of the picture.

Don't cut along the pencil line.

The fairy sticks up at the top.

3. Fill in the fairy with pens. Then, carefully press the point of a sharp pencil through the paper, above the pencil line.

4. Push one scissor blade through the hole. Then, cut carefully around the part of the fairy that is above the pencil line.

5. To make the card stand up, fold the top part back along the pencil line. Then, decorate the card with pens and stickers.

Flower garlands

1. Lay a saucer on some pale pink paper and draw around it. Then, draw around a mug on some bright pink paper.

2. On some white paper, draw around a bottle top. Then, cut out all the circles and glue them together, like this.

To make lots of petals, make more cuts into the circle.

3. For the petals, cut very thin triangles into the biggest circle. Only cut as far as the edge of the bright pink circle.

4. Make more flowers, then cut a drinking straw into short pieces. Tape one piece of straw near the top of each flower.

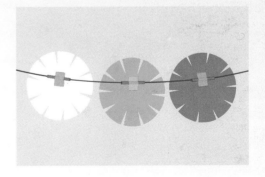

5. With the pieces of straw at the tops of the flowers, thread a long piece of ribbon through them all. Then, hang the flowers up.

Fairy puppets

This side of the wing needs to be on the fold.

1. Fold a piece of thick paper in half. Draw a wing shape on it, like this. Then, keeping the paper folded, cut out the shape.

2. Open out the wings and flatten them. Then, cut a shape for the fairy's body and arms from bright paper.

3. Cut a paper circle for the head and a shape for the hair. Then, glue the hair onto the head and draw a face.

To make your puppets look different, try giving them different dresses and hair.

4. Cut out hands from paper and glue them onto the back of the fairy's arms. Then, glue the head onto the body.

Use pens and stickers to decorate the fairy.

5. Glue the body onto the wings, then decorate the fairy. Turn the fairy over and tape a straw onto the back of the body.

Fairy queen

Make a wand from thick paper and decorate the fairy queen with lots of stickers.

Draw a face.

1. Cut a pair of wings from thick paper and lay them on another piece of paper. Draw bigger wings around them, like this.

2. Cut out the wings and glue the smaller wings onto them. Then, cut a long dress, a head, hair and hands from paper.

3. Glue all the pieces onto the wings. Then, cut a crown from shiny paper and glue it on. Tape a straw onto the back.

Fairyland painting

Toadstools

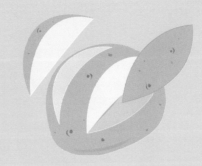

1. Lay some paper towels onto some newspaper. Spread red or pink paint on the paper towels with the back of an old spoon.

2. Cut a potato in half, then carefully cut away the two sides, like this, to make a handle. Press the potato into the paint.

3. Press the potato onto a piece of paper. Then, dip a finger in white paint and print some spots. Using a brush, paint a white stalk.

Daisies and dandelions

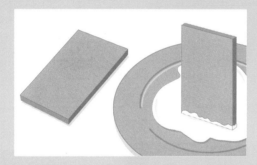

1. Cut two small pieces of thick cardboard. To print daisies, dip the edge of one piece in white paint and press it on the paper.

2. Print lots more lines and cross them over each other, to make petals. Then, paint a yellow dot in the middle of each daisy.

3. Dip the long edge of the other piece of cardboard in yellow paint and print dandelions. Then, paint stalks and leaves.

Dragonflies

1. To paint a body, dip a fingertip into some paint and drag your finger quickly across the paper. Then, fingerpaint a head.

2. Clean your finger, then dip it in some white paint and drag it to make four wings. Then, add eyes with a felt-tip pen.

Add some fingerpainted fairies to your picture. Print their arms and legs with a piece of cardboard.

Print some toadstools first, then add flowers in the spaces.

Butterfly strings

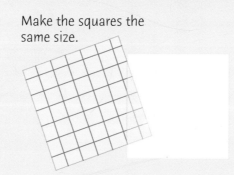

Make the squares the same size.

1. Cut out two squares of clear book covering film. Peel the backing paper off one of the squares, then lay it with the sticky side up.

2. Cut two or three long pieces of thread into lots of little pieces. Cut out lots of pieces of thin material, net and tissue paper, too.

Lay the film sticky-side down.

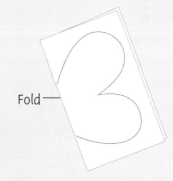

Fold

3. Sprinkle the thread and material over the sticky film. Then, peel the backing paper off the other piece of film and lay it on top.

4. Fold a piece of paper in half. Draw a butterfly wing against the fold and cut it out. Unfold the wings and lay them on the film.

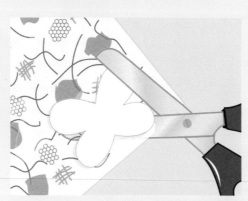

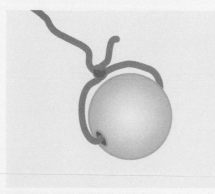

5. Press blobs of poster tack onto the wings. Press the wings onto the film and cut around them. Then, repeat this two more times.

6. Cut a long piece of thread. Push one end of the thread through a bead and tie several knots. Trim the short end off the thread.

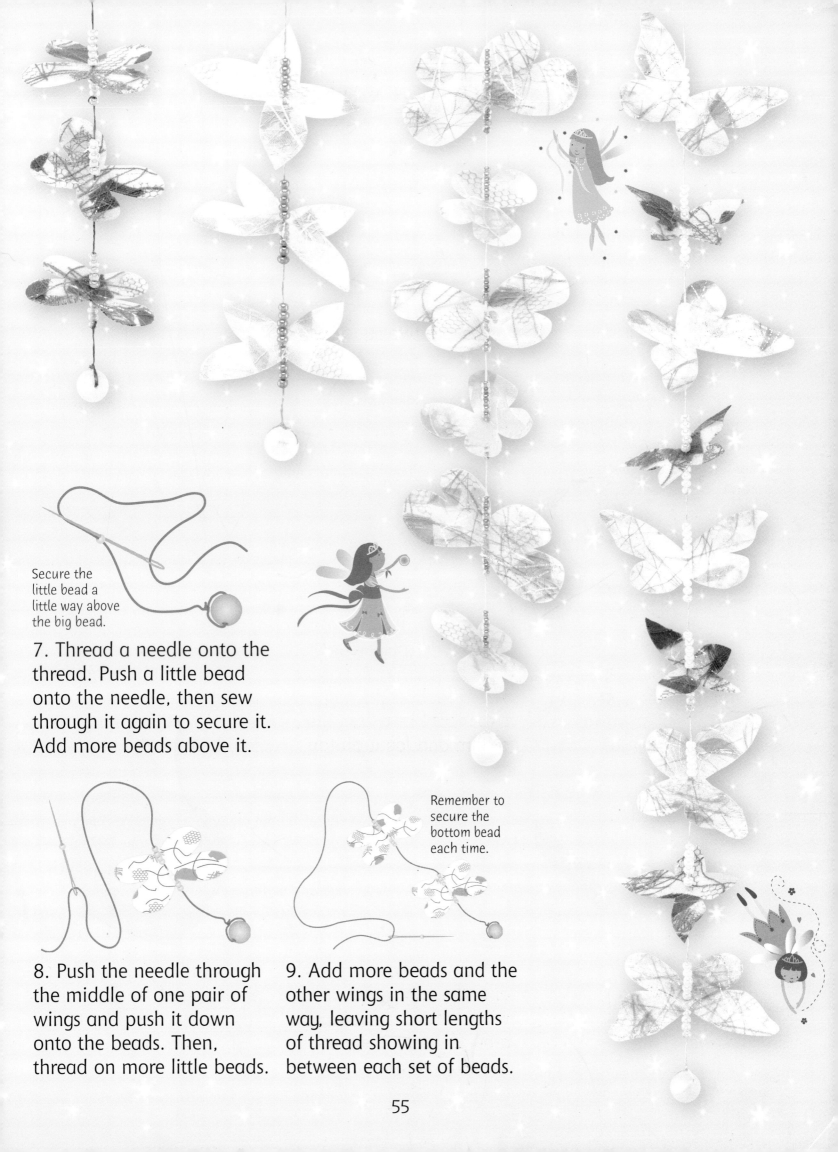

Secure the little bead a little way above the big bead.

7. Thread a needle onto the thread. Push a little bead onto the needle, then sew through it again to secure it. Add more beads above it.

8. Push the needle through the middle of one pair of wings and push it down onto the beads. Then, thread on more little beads.

9. Add more beads and the other wings in the same way, leaving short lengths of thread showing in between each set of beads.

Remember to secure the bottom bead each time.

Love-heart fairies

1. Use a pencil to draw a fairy's head, adding two ears. Draw her hair, eyes, nose and mouth. Draw the dress and add tiny feet.

2. Draw a wing on either side of the dress. Make them look like hearts on their sides. Then, draw arms and hands, on top of the wings.

3. Draw a wand, with the end showing below her fingers. Add some hearts on her dress. Then, draw a heart on top of her head.

Add a band around her head.

Draw the feet near the top of the dress.

Draw a heart on her head, too.

4. Draw around your fairy with a black felt-tip pen. Then, erase the pencil lines. Fill her in with pens. Add hearts near her wand.

5. For a fairy flying sideways, draw an oval head with a nose and an ear. Draw her eye, mouth and hair, then her dress and feet.

6. Draw one arm on the dress and the other one out in front. Add a wand and a heart-shaped wing on her back. Fill her in with pens.

7. Draw a rough circle for a flower. Then, start to draw a spiral inside the circle. Make the lines go near the side of the circle.

8. Continue drawing the spiral, making it overlap or nearly touch the other lines. Finish the spiral with a circle in the middle.

9. Paint the flower with pink paint. Then, fill in some parts with red. When the paint is dry, draw over all the lines with a black pen.

This background was painted in pale pink first. Then, the fairies and flowers were drawn on top when the paint had dried.

If you draw curved lines beside your fairy, they make it look as if she is moving.

Decorate your fairies with lots of hearts on their dresses and in their hair.

Draw lots of leaves around the flowers.

Christmas fairy collage

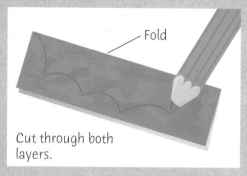

Fold

Cut through both layers.

Join the points in the middle.

1. For the fairy's skirt, rip a shape from pink paper. Don't worry if it's uneven. Glue it onto a piece of paper for the background.

2. For the wings, cut green pictures out of a magazine. Fold them in half and draw half a holly leaf on the fold. Then, cut out the leaves.

3. Unfold the leaves and flatten them. Then, glue them onto the background, just above the top of the fairy's skirt.

4. Rip a shape that is a little bigger than the skirt, from white tissue paper. Then, gather the tissue paper at the top, like this.

You could make a fairy and glue it to the front of a Christmas card.

5. Glue the gathered part of the white tissue paper onto the skirt. Then, cut out a body from white paper and glue it on top.

Use paper from a magazine.

Glue the feet onto some shoes.

Decorate the dress, too.

6. Cut out a head, a neck and some hair. Glue the head and neck onto the hair, then draw a face. Glue the head onto the body.

7. Cut out arms and rip sleeves from paper. Glue them all onto the fairy. Then, cut out feet and glue them on, too.

8. Cut a crown and a strip of paper for a wand and glue them onto the fairy. Add a star sequin or sticker to the end of the wand.

Dancing fairies

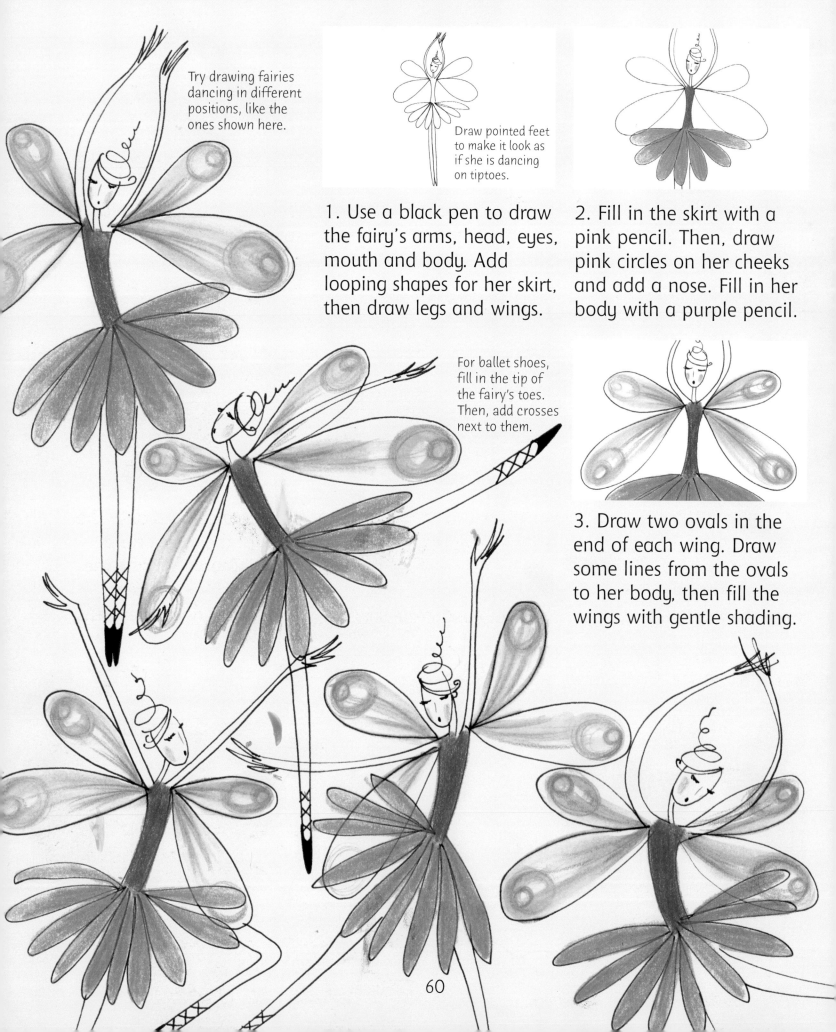

Try drawing fairies dancing in different positions, like the ones shown here.

Draw pointed feet to make it look as if she is dancing on tiptoes.

1. Use a black pen to draw the fairy's arms, head, eyes, mouth and body. Add looping shapes for her skirt, then draw legs and wings.

2. Fill in the skirt with a pink pencil. Then, draw pink circles on her cheeks and add a nose. Fill in her body with a purple pencil.

For ballet shoes, fill in the tip of the fairy's toes. Then, add crosses next to them.

3. Draw two ovals in the end of each wing. Draw some lines from the ovals to her body, then fill the wings with gentle shading.

Glittery bookmark

1. Cut a circle from paper for the fairy's head. Then, draw a shape for the hair on thick pink paper and cut it out.

2. Cover the hair with glue and sprinkle it with glitter. While the glue dries, cut a strip from the pink paper and glue the head onto it.

Use white glue

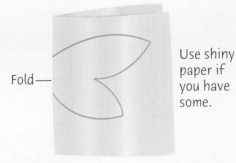

Fold — Use shiny paper if you have some.

3. Glue the hair onto the head and draw a face. Then, cut a crown from shiny paper and glue it onto the hair.

4. For wings, fold a piece of thick paper in half and draw a wing on it, like this. Then, keeping the paper folded, cut out the shape.

5. Glue the wings onto the back of the pink strip of paper. Then, decorate the bookmark with stickers, glitter glue and silver pens.

The shapes on the blue bookmark were drawn with a silver pen.

Fairy slippers

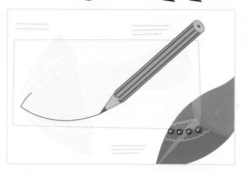

Make sure you press hard.

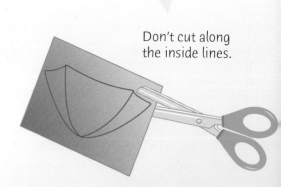

Don't cut along the inside lines.

1. Lay a piece of tracing paper over the template on this page and trace the sole template in pencil. Then, turn the tracing paper over.

2. Lay the tracing paper on a piece of thin cardboard. Draw over the lines to copy them onto the cardboard. Then, cut out the sole.

3. Trace the toe template and copy it onto a piece of thick paper in the same way. Then, cut out the toe shape.

4. Using a ballpoint pen, draw along the lines on the toe. Press hard to make a crease. Then, fold the sides up along the creases.

This is the template for the slipper.

The sole template is shown with a dotted line.

The solid lines show the toe template.

These slippers are for decoration, not for wearing.

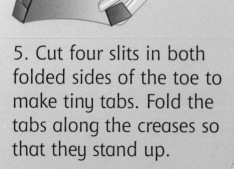

5. Cut four slits in both folded sides of the toe to make tiny tabs. Fold the tabs along the creases so that they stand up.

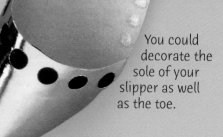

You could decorate the sole of your slipper as well as the toe.

These slippers are shown actual size. You can use them to decorate your room or glue them to cards.

This slipper has a trim made from a cotton ball.

You could use some of the ideas on these slippers to decorate your slipper.

The tabs will overlap each other as you glue them on.

6. Put glue along the front edges of the base of the sole. Then, slide the sole under the right-hand tabs and press them on the glue.

7. With a finger inside the slipper, bend the toe around the sole. Then, press the left-hand tabs onto the glue.

8. Decorate the toe of the slipper with glitter, beads and shiny paper, or draw patterns on it with glitter glue or felt-tip pens.

Mini fairy garland

1. Using a pencil, draw a small heart and a slightly larger one on two shades of pink paper. Then, cut them out.

2. Glue the smaller heart onto the bigger one. Then, using glitter glue, draw around the edge of the smaller heart.

Make your garland from lots of different shapes using ideas from these pages.

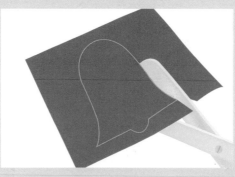

Decorate the glittery side.

3. Brush white glue all over a small piece of bright pink paper. Sprinkle glitter over the top and let the glue dry.

4. When the glue is completely dry, turn the piece of paper over. Draw a bell on the back, then cut it out.

5. Cut a paper shape that will fit across the top of the bell and glue it on. Then, decorate the bell with dots of glitter glue.

Some of these shapes were decorated with sequins and glitter glue.

The tape stops the shapes from sliding down the ribbon.

6. Draw three stars on different shades of purple paper. Cut them out, then glue them together, with the smallest one on top.

7. To hang the shapes, cut pieces of ribbon and fold them in half. Then, tape the ribbons on, to make a loop.

8. Thread the shapes onto a long piece of ribbon and space them out. Then, tape them to the long ribbon with narrow pieces of tape.

Fairy palace

Add extra
decorations to
the palace with
a gold pen.

You could add some
printed fairies from
pages 14-15.

1. Draw a rounded hill on a piece of paper. Draw two more hills, then paint all the hills different shades of green.

2. For the palace, cut a square and two turrets from some paper. Make them small enough to fit on one of the hills.

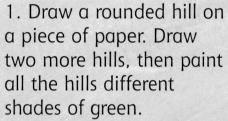

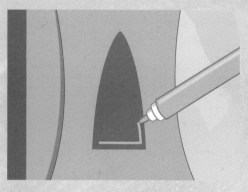

3. Paint a sun and a sky, then glue the palace onto a hill. Then, cut pink paper roofs and glue them onto the palace.

4. Cut windows and doors from paper and glue them onto the palace. Then, draw frames on them with a felt-tip pen.

5. Cut out small paper hearts and glue one on the top of each roof. Then, paint some trees on the background.

6. Cut out photographs of flowers from magazines and glue them onto the background. Then, draw stalks and leaves.

Flowery fairy wall-hanging

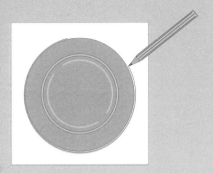

1. Lay a plate on a piece of thick white cardboard. Then, draw around the plate with a pencil and cut out the circle.

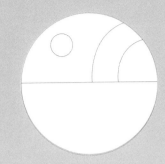

2. Using the pencil, lightly draw a line across the circle. Then, draw the outline of a rainbow and a sun at the top.

3. Add stripes to the rainbow and lots of lines for the sun's rays, like this. Then, paint bright stripes on the rainbow.

4. Paint the sun and its rays with two shades of yellow paint. Then, paint the ground and leave the paint to dry.

5. Draw lots of flowers on white paper, cut them out and paint yellow circles on them. Then, glue some of them onto the ground.

6. Using the point of a ballpoint pen, carefully make a small hole near the top of the painted circle, like this.

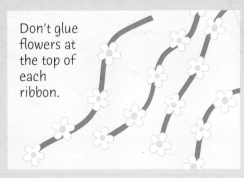

Don't glue flowers at the top of each ribbon.

7. Cut nine long pieces of thin bright ribbon and glue lots of paper flowers onto them. Then, leave the glue to dry.

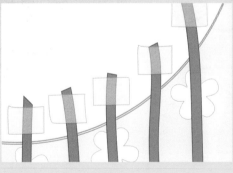

8. Tape the pieces of ribbon around the bottom of the circle, making sure that you leave gaps between them.

9. Thread a piece of ribbon through the hole in the top of the circle, and tie it in a knot. Then, hang up your wall-hanging.

If you don't want to make a hole in your picture, tape a piece of ribbon to the back instead.

You could draw around the outlines with a silver pen or glitter glue.

You can also hang funky fairies on your wall-hanging (see pages 12-13).

Tree-top fairy

1. Lay a plate on some paper and draw around it. Cut out the circle. Then, fold the circle in half and open it out.

Fold

2. Using a pencil, draw a line from the middle of the circle to its edge. Then, draw a wing below the line, touching the fold.

Cut here.

3. Cut up along the fold, around the wing, along the fold again and along the line. Then, cut halfway down the wing, like this.

Line up this edge and the fold.

4. Bend the wing over and gently hold it down, like this. Then, carefully draw around the edge of the wing with a pencil.

Cut here.

5. Open out the paper shape and cut around the second wing. Then, cut halfway down into the wing, like this.

6. Bend the body around so that the cuts in the wings are touching. Slot them together, then curve the body with your hands.

Draw a face.

7. Cut out a head and hair, and glue them together. Cut out arms and glue hands onto them, then glue everything onto the body.

8. Cut out legs and shoes. Draw stripes on the legs, then glue the legs onto the shoes. Then, tape the legs inside the body.

For glittery legs, like these, spread glue on the legs then sprinkle them with glitter.

9. Cut out a crown and a wand from shiny paper and glue them on. Then, decorate the fairy with stickers and sequins.

Spangly star wand

1. Draw a star on a piece of cardboard and cut it out. Then, put the star onto the cardboard again and draw around it.

This wand was made using bits of blue and white tissue paper.

These wands had shiny paper glued around the straw, instead of foil.

Keep the marks at the top of the stars.

The slots need to be the same length.

2. Draw a mark at the top of the first star, then move it off the cardboard. Draw a mark at the top of the second star, then cut it out.

3. Keeping the marks at the top, cut a slot in each star, like this. Make the slots the same thickness as the cardboard.

4. Cut a rectangle from a roll of kitchen foil, making it a little longer and several times wider than a drinking straw.

Squash the end of the straw.

Hold the straw in place.

5. Lay the foil on some old newspaper and cover the non-shiny side with glue. Then, lay the straw on top, near one edge of the foil.

6. Roll the straw, so that the foil sticks all the way around it. Then, tape the straw onto the star with a slot at the top.

7. Hold the star with the slot at the bottom, above the star with the slot at the top. Then, push the stars together, like this.

Use white glue.

8. Rip up lots of strips of tissue paper and glue them all over the stars. Cover the stars with two or three layers of tissue paper.

9. Brush the stars with glue and sprinkle them with glitter. Glue on lots of beads and sequins, or shapes cut from shiny paper.

Flying fairies scene

To make a picture like this, paint toadstools and a fairy castle, then add fairies and flowers.

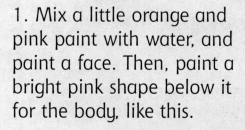

1. Mix a little orange and pink paint with water, and paint a face. Then, paint a bright pink shape below it for the body, like this.

2. Paint two paler shapes for the fairy's wings. Then, paint a yellow shape for the hair and a circle for the wand.

3. Leave the paint to dry completely. Then, use a black felt-tip pen to add outlines to the fairy's head, body and wings.

More ideas

Piled-up

Spiky

Wavy

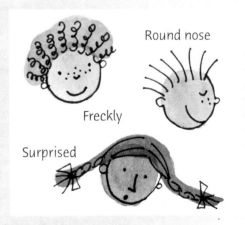

Round nose

Freckly

Surprised

4. Draw a face, then add arms, legs and lines on the fairy's hair. Then, draw a wand with a star on the end, like this.

Try painting different hairstyles. Paint a tall shape for piled-up hair, zigzags for spiky hair and curly lines for wavy hair.

Try different faces, too. A few dots make freckles, a round mouth looks surprised and noses can be round or pointed.

Fairy tiara

Only cut halfway into the band.

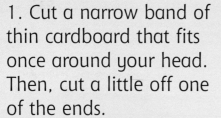

1. Cut a narrow band of thin cardboard that fits once around your head. Then, cut a little off one of the ends.

2. A little way from one end, make a cut going down into the band. Then, make a second cut going up into the other end.

3. Cut six strips of kitchen foil which are twice as wide as the band. Then, squeeze and roll them to make thin sticks.

You could use shiny cardboard for the band.

You can bend the foil sticks in lots of different ways to make different kinds of tiaras.

Try hanging a paper heart from a piece of thread.

The tiara sits on the top of your head. You may need to clip it to your hair.

Leave some space at each end of the band.

4. Cut each stick in half. Then, bend one piece in half so that it makes an arch. Tape it onto the middle of the band.

5. Bend the rest of the foil sticks and tape five arches on either side of the middle one. Then, turn the tiara over.

6. Decorate the front of the tiara with stickers and sequins. Then, slot its ends together so that the ends are inside, like this.

77

Fairy collage

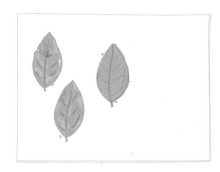

Use paint that isn't too runny.

1. For the wings, lay a small leaf onto some newspaper, with the veins facing up. Then, brush paint over the leaf.

2. Lay the leaf on a piece of tissue paper and press hard all over it with your fingertips. Print six more leaves and let them dry.

You may need to overlap the leaves.

3. Cut out all the printed leaves. Then, cut a pale paper circle for a head. Cut some hair for the fairy from shiny paper.

4. Glue the hair onto the head, and add a face. Then, from bright paper, cut a top and a skirt for the fairy's dress.

5. Glue the skirt onto the top. Then, glue three printed leaves onto the skirt. Cut a strip of paper for a sash, and glue it on.

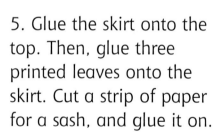

6. From pale paper, cut two arms and glue them to the back of the body. Then, glue on four leaves for the fairy's wings.

7. Turn the body over and glue it onto a piece of paper, but don't glue the bottom of the skirt yet. Then, glue on the head.

8. Cut two shoes from shiny paper and glue them just under the fairy's skirt. Glue the bottom of the skirt onto the paper.

You can use any bright or shiny paper, such as wrapping paper, for the dress.

Make fairies with different hairstyles and crowns.

To make a layered skirt, cut an extra layer and glue it underneath.

9. Cut a crown and a wand from shiny paper and glue them on. Then, decorate the fairy with lots of shiny stickers.

Hanging hearts

Keep the material folded.

1. Draw a heart on a piece of thin paper and cut it out. Fold a piece of material in half, pin the heart onto it and cut around it.

Use a pin to secure the small heart.

2. Cut out a smaller heart from another piece of material. Sew it in the middle of one of the big hearts with running stitch.

3. Tie a bow in a piece of thin ribbon. Sew it onto the hearts with several little stitches through the middle of the knot.

4. Pin the two big hearts together. Sew around the edges with running stitch, but leave a gap at the top, like this.

5. Twist one end of a pipe cleaner around to make a spiral. Then, twist the other end in the opposite direction, like this.

6. Push the pipe cleaner into the gap. Then, tear a cotton ball into pieces and push them inside the heart. Don't fill it too full.

Use the pipecleaner to hang up your stitched heart.

7. Continue to sew around the edge of the heart with running stitch. Then, finish off by doing one or two tiny stitches.

81

Fairy heart card

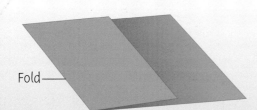

Fold

1. To make the card, fold a long rectangle of thick paper, like this. The front part should be narrower than the back part.

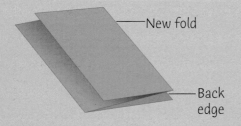

New fold

Back edge

2. Turn the paper over. Then, fold back the right-hand section, so that the new fold lines up with the back edge of the card.

You could decorate a tall card with a big heart and sequins.

Try adding extra sparkle with glitter glue.

Glue hearts along more than one edge of a card.

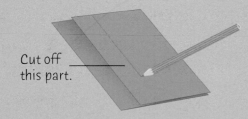

Cut off this part.

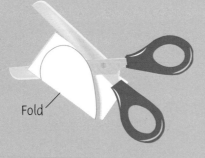

Fold

3. The front section should be about half of the width of the card. If it's wider, draw a pencil line down the card and cut along it.

4. To make the heart decorations, fold a piece of thick paper in half. Draw half a heart against the fold, then cut it out.

5. Open out the heart. Lay it on a piece of pink paper and draw around it. Then, draw around it twice more on other pieces of paper.

You could decorate a card with a flower made from hearts.

The little heart in the middle was brushed with glue and sprinkled with glitter.

This card had different shades of paper glued inside and on the front.

Only glue the left side of each heart.

6. Cut out the hearts. Then, cut out another smaller heart from thick paper. Draw around it three times and cut out the shapes.

7. Glue one small heart onto each big heart. Then, glue the big hearts along the edge on the front of the card, like this.

8. Brush lots of dots of white glue around the edges of the hearts and press on sequins. Then, leave the glue to dry.

Moonlight fairies

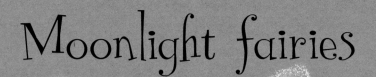

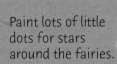
Paint lots of little dots for stars around the fairies.

Use chalk or a chalk pastel.

1. Cut a triangular-shaped skirt from white tissue paper, then rip it along the bottom. Glue the skirt onto a piece of dark blue paper.

2. Use white chalk to draw the top layer of the skirt on top of the tissue paper. Draw some white lines inside as the pleats in her skirt.

3. Cut another piece of tissue paper for the body and glue it on. Draw the fairy's wings in white chalk on either side of the body.

4. Rub the chalk to smudge the wings. This will make them look transparent. Then, draw around them again and add lines inside.

5. Paint the fairy's neck and head, then paint two thin lines for arms. Then, paint lots of wavy lines for the fairy's hair.

For a glowing moon, draw a circle with chalk and smudge it with your finger. Then, paint the middle with yellow paint.

6. Draw a line with white chalk for the wand. Then, paint several little yellow lines coming out from the end of it, for a star.

7. When the paint is completely dry, draw her eyes, nose and lips with felt-tip pens. Add little pink ovals on her cheeks.

If you draw the fairies at different angles it will make them look as if they are flying.

Sparkly heart strings

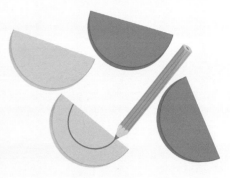

1. Place a mug on a piece of pink paper. Draw around it twice and cut out the circles. Then, cut two circles from purple paper, too.

2. Fold all the circles in half. On one circle, draw a half-circle. Then, keeping the paper folded, cut along the line you have drawn.

3. Keeping the small piece folded, draw the shape of half a heart against the fold. Then, carefully cut along the line.

4. Lay the large 'C' shape on a folded circle and draw around the inside. Draw around it again on the other circles. Cut along the lines.

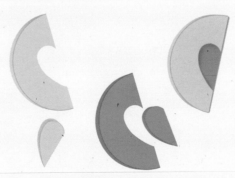

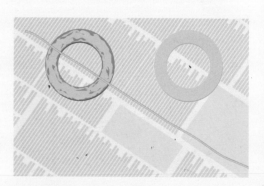

5. Lay the piece with the heart cut out on a folded circle. Draw around the heart and cut it out. Do the same with the other circles.

6. Open out the shapes. Spread glue on a pink ring, then lay a long piece of thread over it. Press a purple ring on top.

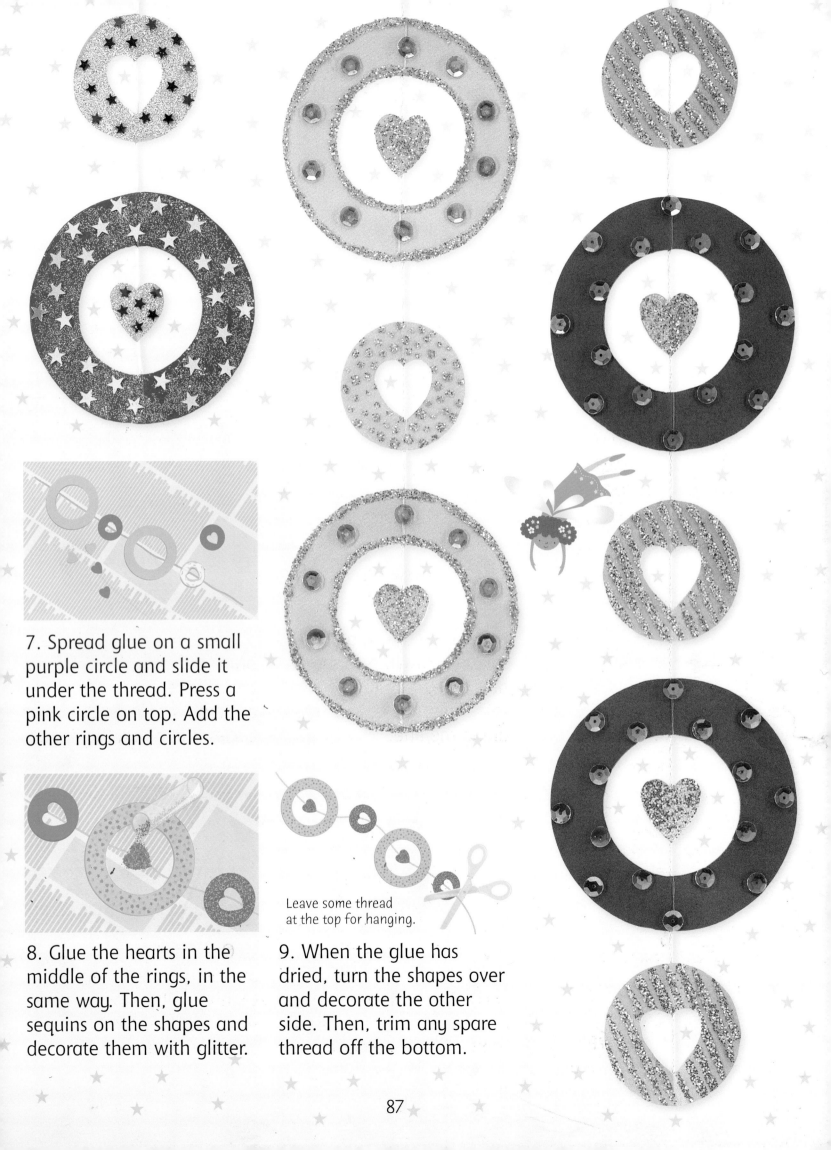

7. Spread glue on a small purple circle and slide it under the thread. Press a pink circle on top. Add the other rings and circles.

8. Glue the hearts in the middle of the rings, in the same way. Then, glue sequins on the shapes and decorate them with glitter.

9. When the glue has dried, turn the shapes over and decorate the other side. Then, trim any spare thread off the bottom.

Leave some thread at the top for hanging.

Fairy cakes

Use the ideas shown in this picture for decorating your fairies and cakes.

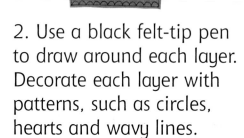

Make each layer smaller than the one below.

Add more hearts and spots with the gold pen.

1. Cut a rectangle of tissue paper for the bottom layer of a cake. Glue it onto some paper. Then, cut more layers and glue them on.

2. Use a black felt-tip pen to draw around each layer. Decorate each layer with patterns, such as circles, hearts and wavy lines.

3. Draw some holders for candles. Then, cut candles from tissue paper and glue them on. Add flames with a gold felt-tip pen.

You could draw fairies doing different things, such as lighting a candle or carrying a cherry.

You could decorate a cake with tissue paper cherries.

Draw a wavy line along the bottom of the dress.

Fill in the wand with the gold pen, too.

4. Cut a shape from tissue paper for a fairy's dress. Glue it near the cake. Cut two pairs of wings and glue them next to the dress.

5. Use a black pen to draw around the dress and the wings. Add her arms below the wings, a neck and a curve for the chin.

6. Use a gold pen to draw the fairy's hair. Then, draw her face and add a wand. Decorate the dress, and her legs, with the gold pen.

Hang the fairies on a tree with lots of other decorations.

Fairy tree decorations

Use a silver pen if you have one.

1. Draw around a mug on some paper. Cut out the circle, then fold it in half. Then, unfold the circle and cut along the fold.

2. Draw two arms on one of the half-circles and cut them out. Decorate them with a pen. Then, cut out hands and glue them on.

3. For the body, decorate the second half-circle. Then, to make it into a cone, glue halfway along its straight edge.

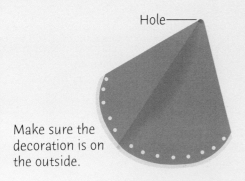

Hole

Make sure the decoration is on the outside.

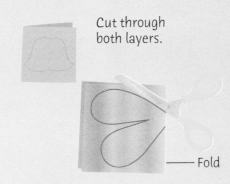

Cut through both layers.

Fold

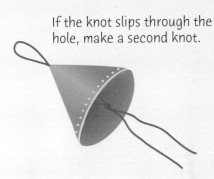

4. Bend the paper around and press the straight edges together until they stick. Then, cut off the top of the cone, to make a tiny hole.

5. Fold two pieces of paper in half. Draw hair on one and draw a wing on the other, touching the fold. Then, cut out the shapes.

6. Draw a face and cut it out. Glue it onto one of the hair shapes. Then, cut a long piece of thread and fold it in half.

If the knot slips through the hole, make a second knot.

7. Halfway down the piece of thread, tie a knot, to make a loop. Then, push the loop through the hole in the top of the body.

8. Glue the arms onto the body. Glue the loop onto the back part of the hair, then glue the face on top. Glue on the wings.

9. For shoes, thread small beads onto the two pieces of thread hanging down. Then, tie knots below the beads to secure them.

Fairyland flowers

1. Fold a piece of tissue paper in half. Place a mug on top and draw around it. Then, keeping the paper folded, cut out the circle.

2. Lay both circles of tissue paper on some newspaper. Then, dab white glue around their edges and sprinkle glitter on top.

Make lots of flowers, then twist the stems together to make one plant.

3. When the glue is dry, gently push one end of a sparkly pipe cleaner through the middle of both circles to make a stem.

4. Slide the circles a little way down the stem. Then, firmly pinch the tissue paper and twist it around the stem.

5. Wrap a small piece of sticky tape around the tissue paper and stem, to secure them. Push the petals open a little, if you need to.

6. To make a leaf, fold another piece of tissue paper in half. Draw a leaf shape, then cut it out, keeping the paper folded.

You could use different shades of tissue paper for the flowers.

7. Cut another pipe cleaner in half. Spread glue over one of the leaves, then press one end of the pipe cleaner onto the glue.

8. While the glue is still wet, gently press the other leaf on top. Then, spread glue over the leaf and sprinkle it with glitter.

9. When the glue is dry, lay the stem of the leaf next to the flower stem. Tightly twist them together, then bend the leaf out.

Fairy paperchain

Make several fairy chains
and tape them together to
make long chains, like these.

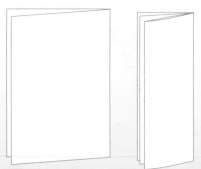

1. Fold a long rectangle of
thin paper in half, so that
the shorter edges meet.
Then, fold the paper in half
again. Crease the folds well.

2. Draw a fairy's dress and
arms on the folded paper,
making sure that the arms
touch each side of the paper.
Draw a shape for the hair.

3. Cut around your drawing,
but don't cut along the folds
along her hands. Then,
unfold the paper to make a
chain of four fairies.

These fairies were decorated with shapes cut from paper and a gold pen, too.

You could cut a star from foil instead of a fairy crown.

Cut out foil crowns and glue them on, too.

4. Fill in the fairies with felt-tip pens. Then, draw four faces on a separate piece of paper. Cut them out and glue them onto the fairies.

5. Draw stripes across the dresses with pens. Then, cut strips of patterned paper from magazines and glue them onto the dresses.

6. Fold a piece of kitchen foil following step 1. Draw wings against the fold. Cut them out and glue them onto the fairies' backs.

Index

Images of flowers on pages 20-21 and 66-67 © Digital Vision.
First published in 2006 by Usborne Publishing Ltd., 83-85 Saffron Hill, London, EC1N 8RT, England. www.usborne.com Copyright © 2006, 2003. Usborne
Publishing Ltd. The name Usborne and the devices ♀ ⊕ are Trade Marks of Usborne Publishing Ltd. All rights reserved. No part of this publication may be
reproduced, stored in a retrieval system, or transmitted in any form or by any means, electronic, mechanical, photocopying, recording or otherwise, without the
prior permission of the publisher. First published in America in 2006. UE. Printed in Malaysia.